F
Gra   Gray, Genevieve
         STRAY.

D0266523

STRAY

STRAY

By
GENEVIEVE GRAY

Illustrations by
NAN BROOKS

EMC Corporation
St. Paul, Minnesota

F
GRA

Library of Congress Cataloging in Publication Data

Gray, Genevieve S
  Stray.

  (Her Girl stuff series)
  SUMMARY: Marianne is followed about by a strange dog at
school much to the dismay of her teachers.
  [1. Dogs — Stories.   2. School stories]
I. Brooks, Nan, illus.   II. Title.
PZ7.G7774St   [Fic]   73-4587
ISBN 0-912022-66-3
ISBN 0-912022-67-1 (pbk)

GIRL STUFF SERIES

HOT SHOT
BREAK-IN
STRAY
STAND-OFF

"Hey, Marianne," called Linda. "Who's your friend?"

Marianne turned and frowned. Following at her heels was a mongrel dog with a shaggy coat the color of wet cement. "He's no friend of mine!" Marianne answered.

As soon as she had arrived at school that morning, the dog had run to meet her, bounding like a rabbit on his long haunches and short forelegs. Now he gazed up at her from little red eyes set in a head shaped like an oatmeal box. His long, rat-like tail wagged so hard it threw him off balance. He flopped his hind quarters to one side like a walrus and sat down.

Marianne shook her head. "Man alive! What an ugly mutt!"

"Wooooooooo!" replied the dog.

"Listen to him," said Linda. "He wails like a siren."

"Woooooooooo!" agreed the dog.

"He can't run right, he can't sit right, he can't even bark right," observed Marianne. "Talk about a dopey dog!"

"I wonder who he belongs to," said Linda. Marianne ran her fingers through the wiry fur at the animal's neck, hunting a collar and dog tags. She found nothing.

"That's no surprise," scoffed Linda. "If I owned a dog like that, I wouldn't want the news to get around either."

Just then the school bell rang. From all over the school ground, boys and girls streamed toward the big building to begin classes for the day.

The dog got to his feet and trotted along with them as if he intended to go to school too. He was soon lost in the crowd of students at the entrance.

"That proves it," said Linda. "Only a real dope would go to school if he didn't have to."

"He's in for a disappointment," said Marianne. "No dogs allowed. He'll get kicked out, but fast."

In class ten minutes later, Mr. Goodman was putting up some charts for science. Marianne heard a faint clicking sound, such as a dog's claws might make walking on a hard floor. The sound came closer and stopped beside Marianne's desk. And there was the dog.

All around Marianne the kids leaned out of their seats to stare and giggle. Mr. Goodman turned and stared too.

"Is that your dog, Marianne?"

"No, sir."

"Whose is it, then?"

"I don't know."

"Take him outside, will you please?"

"Come on, you," Marianne said. The dog trotted obediently after Marianne through the classroom door and down the long hall to the outside entrance. Marianne held the door open. "Out!" she ordered. The mongrel avoided her gaze and slunk out, tail between his legs, as though he had been whipped. Marianne returned to class.

At recess, Claudia and Josie walked outside with Marianne. "It's lucky Mrs. Elrod
didn't catch you with that dog," said
Claudia.

"It's not my dog," Marianne protested.

"That doesn't matter," said Josie. "Mrs.
Elrod got bitten by a dog once. Real bad.
She hates dogs like poison. You'd be in bad
with her all year long."

"Just on account of old Dopey?"
Marianne was indignant. "I don't care if
Mrs. Elrod is principal of Robertson School.
She's got no right to take out her spite on
a poor old dumb dog!"

They had filed out the school ground
entrance, and no sooner were the words out
of Marianne's mouth than a bundle of gray
fur hit her behind the knees. She nearly
toppled, taking Claudia down with her, but
caught herself in time.

"Why you ornery pooch, you!" Marianne cried. "What a dirty trick!"

The mongrel scampered in happy circles, ready for a romp. "Woooooo!" he moaned invitingly. He looked so comical, Marianne laughed in spite of herself.

"I wonder if he knows how to fetch," she said with grudging affection. In the pocket of her jacket she found one of her gloves and threw it. The dog was off in an instant, bouncing across the ground on his big hind legs.

Claudia watched him curiously. "Gee, that dog's built funny," she said. "He looks like he started out in front to be a terrier and ended up in back being a greyhound."

"Honestly!" protested Marianne. "Everybody says mean things about poor old Dopey Dog. I feel sorry for him."

The mongrel returned with the glove in his mouth and laid it at Marianne's feet. "Woooooo," he bleated, and thrashed his rope-like tail so hard he whacked the girls on the shins.

"Funny old pooch," murmured Marianne, scratching the ruff at the animal's neck. Then she threw the glove again and the dog was off.

"If you like him so much, why don't you keep him?" suggested Josie. "He likes you, too. Anybody can tell that."

"He doesn't have a dog collar or tags," said Claudia. "Maybe he doesn't belong to anybody at all. Why not adopt him?"

Marianne liked the idea. "Hmm," she mused. "I'd have to do some tall talking at home. Mom would throw a fit if I brought home an ugly mutt like that. Or at least she would till she got used to him."

"You could walk him home at noon," suggested Claudia.

"Yeah," Marianne said, "if he's still here at noon. But what if he runs away?"

"Maybe if we got him a box to stay in," suggested Claudia. "We could hide it under the bushes next to the building. He'd be warm there, out of the wind."

"Ha!" scoffed Josie. "And just where are we going to get a box?"

"Miss Lawson has lots, down in her room. She's got her second-graders building a grocery store or something."

They all groaned. Miss Glorabelle Lawson was two hundred pounds of solid muscle and her normal speaking voice could be heard a block away if the wind was right. The older kids were scared of her. The month before, Miss Lawson had caught a sixth-grade boy teasing one of her second-graders. Miss Lawson picked up the boy by the scruff of the neck and carried him to the office like a satchel. "Forget it," said Josie.

"Maybe if I make him a warm bed with my jacket," Marianne said. "Then maybe he'll stick around so I can find him later. It won't hurt to try, will it?"

They found a sheltered spot under the shrubbery. Marianne hollowed out a spot in some leaves, lining it with her jacket. The dog crept into the nest, curled up, and lay down with a contented grunt. But when Marianne started to leave, he rolled his bloodshot eyes up at her anxiously and rose to follow.

"Stay there, Dopey Dog," ordered Marianne.

"Wooooooo!" mourned the dog.

And then recess was over. Marianne gave the mongrel a final pat on the head and followed the others back inside to class. Mr. Goodman had started everyone on the morning's reading assignment when Marianne again heard the click of Dopey's claws on the floor. She sighed.

This time Mr. Goodman was angry. "Marianne, I thought I told you before to put that mutt outside!"

"I did, Mr. Goodman," said Marianne. "I guess somebody let him in again."

"That somebody wasn't you, was it?" Mr. Goodman glared.

"No, Mr. Goodman," Marianne protested. "I didn't let him in."

This time Dopey Dog wasn't as willing to leave as he had been earlier. Marianne tried to pick him up.

But Dopey slid in six directions at once. His bones seemed to have turned to molasses.

"Want me to help, Mr. Goodman?" Linda volunteered from her seat two rows away.

"Maybe you'd better. Looks as if the animal has come apart at the seams."

Linda helped Marianne haul Dopey out of the classroom. Outside in the hall, Linda whispered, "I've got an idea. None of the teachers ever go in the girls' restroom. Let's put him in there."

"You're crazy," protested Marianne. "He'll get out and come right back. Anyway, the janitor goes in the restroom every morning to clean up. He'll find Dopey!"

"Mr. Bowers?" said Linda. "Mr. Bowers is a good sport. He won't tell. And anyway, we'll put up a sign."

"What kind of a sign?" asked Marianne in a skeptical voice.

"Come on," said Linda. "I'll show you."

Together they carried Dopey down the hall to the girls' restroom. Linda pulled a paper towel from the wall container. Then she tore off a corner of a second paper towel and rolled it into a short, thin pencil. She cupped her hand under the soap dispenser and pushed the release button until there was a little pool of bright green soap in her palm. Dipping the paper into the green soap Linda carefully printed on the paper towel, "DON'T LET THE DOG OUT."

"Hey, that's neat," said Marianne. "Now that you've got the sign, how are you going to put it up where kids can read it?"

"Good question," replied Linda, looking around the room.

"Maybe if you tore the paper towel across the top so there was a hook," suggested Marianne. "Maybe it would hook on one of the door handles. Then the kids would be sure to read it as soon as they came in."

They tried it and it worked. Marianne turned and stroked Dopey's shaggy neck. "You be good, Dopey, do you hear?"

"Wooooooo. . ."

Marianne clamped his muzzle shut. She glared into his little pink eyes.

"Sh-h-h!" she commanded and hurriedly they left.

Back in class, Marianne squirmed through the next hour until lunch time. At last the noon bell rang, and kids swarmed out of their classrooms into the halls. Marianne and Linda headed for the restroom.

"With the hall crowded with kids, we can sneak him out easy," said Linda. "Then you can walk him home. You'll get back in plenty of time."

Inside the restroom their eyes fell on the sign they had left earlier. Beside it was another sign, neatly printed with a black felt pen and held in place with tape. It said, "To the person who left this note: Our school restrooms are not to be used as kennels. The dog you left has no collar and no evidence of rabies shots. The dog is outside on the school ground. I have phoned the City Pound to come pick him up. Mrs. Elrod."

"Ohhhhhh," moaned Marianne.

"Stop groaning and come on," Linda said. "Maybe we can find him."

Linda went to get Claudia and Josie to help hunt. All four girls raced outside.

They looked everywhere — under the bushes beside the building, under the cars in the parking lot, in the stairwell that led to the basement door. Dopey was nowhere to be found.

"The dog catcher already came and got him," whimpered Marianne. Tears began to gather in her eyes. "He took my dog."

"Aw, Marianne," said Linda. "It wasn't really your dog anyway."

"Get your mother to take you to the Dog Pound after school," suggested Claudia. "Then you can get him back. He'll be there. You wait and see."

"Let's go eat lunch," said Josie with a sigh.

After lunch they stood talking on the school ground. Out of the corner of her eye, Marianne suddenly saw a streak of gray.

Then something hit the back of her legs.
This time the blow sent her sprawling.

"Dopey!" she cried joyously, and she
gathered the wiggling mutt in her arms.

"I hate to interrupt," said Josie dryly,
"but do you see what I see?"

Rolling down the street toward them was
a white panel truck. Painted on the side was
"CITY POUND".

Not far away from the girls were several
big cement pipes that served as part of
Robertson School's playground equipment.
Josie jerked her head toward them.
"Quick!" she ordered. "Inside!"

Marianne dragged Dopey into one of the big pipes. Claudia crawled in behind her and Linda crept in at the other end. Josie stationed herself outside to keep watch and to chase away curious bystanders.

A few minutes passed. Josie stooped and looked inside. "The guy parked his truck in front of the building," she reported. "Now he's coming out on the school ground. Pretend you're looking for something."

Just then they heard a man's voice call, "Hey, you kids over there!"

Josie called back, "You mean us?"

"Yeah," came the man's voice. "Have you kids seen a dirty white dog anywhere?"

"No, we sure haven't," Josie called.

"He's supposed to be here on the school ground someplace."

"We haven't seen any white dog," Josie insisted. "If we do, though, we'll let you know."

A moment later, Josie clambered into the pipe on top of Claudia. "He's leaving. A few minutes more and he'll be gone."

"Josie, you told a lie," Claudia accused her.

Josie was indignant. "I did not tell a lie. You heard the guy. 'A dirty white dog,' he said. Dopey isn't a dirty white dog, he's a gray dog."

"Hey, Josie, you know what?" said Linda. "The bell's going to ring in a minute and Marianne hasn't taken Dopey home yet."

"So let her get a belly ache or something," said Josie. "Why can't she get sick and take the dog home and not come back this afternoon?"

Marianne cocked her head sarcastically. "My mother caught on to that trick before I was out of first grade. Try again."

Just then, sure enough, the bell rang. At the same moment a paper napkin blew across the school ground not far from the pipe. It caught Dopey's eye and the dog streaked after it before Marianne could hold him. The girls started after him but Claudia stopped them. "Skreeeeeks!" she gasped. "Look over there by the fence! Old Lady Elrod!"

"And Mr. Bowers," added Linda.

And then Mrs. Elrod spied Dopey. "Mr. Bowers!" she cried. "I knew that filthy dog must still be around here somewhere! There he is! Catch him!"

The breeze tumbled the paper napkin end over end and Dopey leaped after it. A sudden gust blew the napkin farther away.

It landed in the area where the teachers' cars were parked. By the time Mr. Bowers collected his wits and ran after Dopey, the dog had disappeared among the cars.

"Oh, glug!" moaned Josie. "Now he's done it, for sure."

"Where did he go?" asked Claudia. "Did you see where he went?"

"Yeah, I saw." Josie's voice sounded flat.

"So did I," said Marianne in despair. "He jumped into one of the cars."

"He did?" asked Claudia. "Which one?"

"Miss Lawson's," said Josie.

Stunned into silence, the girls crossed the school ground. They entered the school building without another word.

After noon period Marianne tried to get her mind on fractions and decimals, but she couldn't. During afternoon recess Josie sneaked a look in Miss Lawson's car to see if Dopey was still there, but he wasn't. He wasn't on the school ground and he wasn't hiding in the pipes.

Later, when Mrs. McDonald took the class to the auditorium for music, Marianne couldn't get her mind on singing either. Mrs. McDonald started off the music class by having everybody sing "America, the Beautiful." They had finished the first part and were into the chorus when Marianne heard it.

"Wooooooooooo."

". . . and crown thy good with brotherhood, from sea to shining sea," sang the students.

"WOOOOOOOOOO!" Everybody froze.

"Woooooooo. WOOOOOOOOOOOO!"

It was a scary sound, like a phantom floating around in the shadows backstage.

Mrs. McDonald went to investigate. In a moment they heard her stern voice ask, "Whose dog is this in the costume closet?"

"It's Marianne's dog!" someone called.

"Marianne! Come get this beast and put it outside immediately!" Mrs. McDonald ordered.

"Yes, Mrs. McDonald," said Marianne.

Dopey was overjoyed to see Marianne again. He tried to lick both of her hands at once and wiggled so hard that she could scarcely pick him up.

Marianne was still struggling with Dopey when the school bell unexpectedly sounded three long blasts. Mrs. McDonald sighed impatiently, then announced, "Fire drill, boys and girls. Line up and file out the door behind the stage. Then we'll march around to the side of the building with the others."

"What do you want me to do about the dog, Mrs. McDonald?" asked Marianne.

"Bring him along."

They paraded out two by two, Marianne bringing up the rear with Josie helping to carry Dopey. His tail and long hind legs flopped like a broken kite as the girls struggled to carry him.

The music class students rounded the corner of the building. "Yikes!" exclaimed Josie. For who should be standing there, directing the students as they streamed out the big double doors, but Mrs. Elrod!

Out of the corner of her mouth, Josie muttered to Marianne, "Her back's turned. Act like nothing's wrong and maybe she won't see us."

On they marched, nearer and nearer to Mrs. Elrod. Marianne held her breath. And then they were safely past and taking their places beside the younger children already lined up on the sidewalk. Dopey drew admiring glances from the smaller children. They turned to pat him and scratch his ears.

Marianne and Josie hardly had time to sigh with relief over their narrow escape before they were suddenly startled out of their wits.

"Just one minute there, girls," thundered a mighty voice behind them. *"What do you think you're doing with my dog?"*

They turned. Bearing down upon them like a mother elephant protecting her young was Miss Glorabelle Lawson!

"Ww-w-w . . ." stammered Marianne. Josie gulped.

And then, before their astonished eyes, tough old Miss Lawson took the scruffy dog in her huge arms and began to talk to him. "Naughty Twigs," crooned Miss Lawson. "Twigs played a trick on Mother, didn't he? Got out of the house this morning without his collar, didn't he? And hid in the back seat of Mother's car. You're a naughty Twigsie. Yes, you are."

Miss Lawson scowled down at Josie and Marianne. "I'm going to put Twigs in my car where he'll be safe for the afternoon.

Help the other teachers keep an eye on my second-graders until I get back. And no monkey business! Understand?"

"Yes, Miss Lawson," said Marianne.

"Sure, Miss Lawson," said Josie. "Whatever you say."

Miss Lawson quickly returned. But before Marianne had a chance to explain, the fire drill was over and everyone was filing back inside.

Next day when Marianne told Miss Lawson the whole story, Miss Lawson nearly fainted. "The City Pound!" she cried, horrified. "I knew Mrs. Elrod didn't like dogs, but I had no idea she'd . . . Good heavens! Twigs might have been picked up and I'd never have known what happened to him! What a close call *that* was!"

Miss Lawson dabbed at her forehead with a handkerchief. Her voice trembled as she said how grateful she was to Marianne for saving Twigs. "Yes, Twigs is only a mongrel," she admitted, "and an ugly mongrel at that. But Twigs has character. I'm glad you saw that, Marianne. Only people with truly noble hearts can appreciate animals because of their character and not their looks." Then Miss Lawson blew her nose. It sounded like the blast of a diesel locomotive. Marianne decided that Miss Lawson must have a pretty soft heart underneath all that muscle, no matter what the older kids said about her.

The next Saturday morning a messenger delivered a wire dog cage with a big red bow tied on top. There was a card that said, "With thanks, Glorabelle Lawson."

Inside the cage was a puppy. It had a pug nose like a bulldog and four skinny stilts for legs. It had short black-and-white fur except for patches of longer, yellowish fur on its back. The puppy looked like an old toy animal whose yellow insides were spilling out here and there.

"You *ugly* pooch!" exclaimed Marianne.

"Woooooo!" said the puppy.

Marianne named him Dopey.